D0100254

# The Rainforest Race

adapted by Lara Bergen    based on the teleplay by Rosemary Contreras
illustrated by Corey Wolfe and Art Mawhinney

Hi, I am Diego! Today is the Rainforest Race!
I love races! Do you?

There are animal teams from all over the rainforest. There is a spectacled bear team, a howler monkey team, and a puma team.

The winner of the race will get a big, blue ribbon.

Armadillo wants to be in the race too. But she does not have a team.

Armadillo is worried. The other animals are bigger.

But Armadillo has a strong shell. She has sharp claws. And she can roll into a ball. The other animals cannot do that!

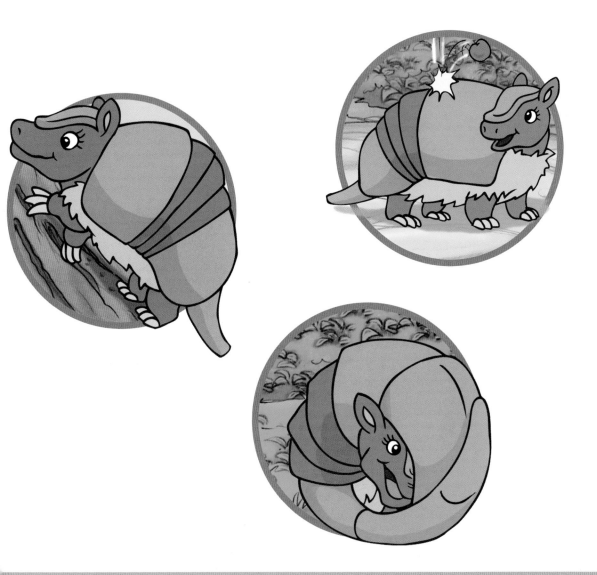

It is time to start the race! We need to go to the shaky nut trees, the muddy mud slide, and the big mountain.

Here are the shaky nut trees! The nuts are slowing the big animals down.

But Armadillo has a strong shell. The nuts do not stop her.
Go, Armadillo, go!

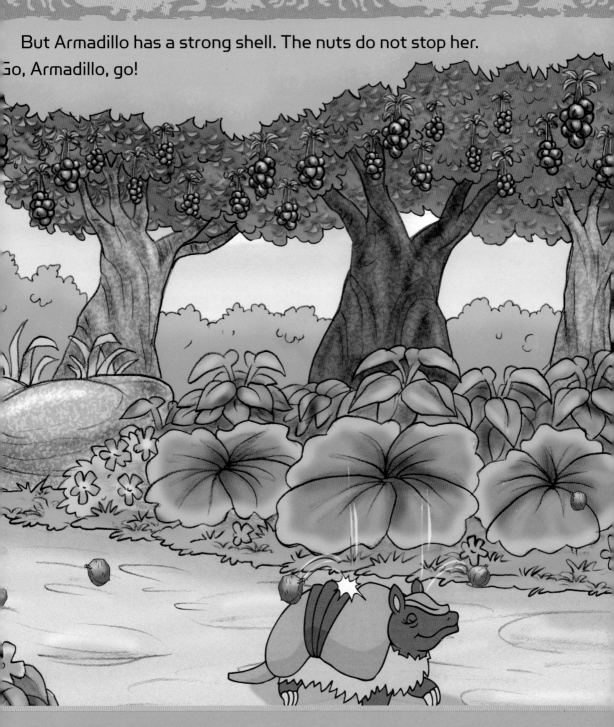

Now we are at the muddy mud slide. The pumas, the spectacled bears, and the howler monkeys slide down.

Oh, no!  Armadillo cannot slide. Her short legs are stuck in the mud.

But Armadillo can roll into a ball. Armadillo can roll down the muddy mud slide. Roll, Armadillo, roll!

We made it to the big mountain.
The other teams are at the top.

Armadillo is at the bottom. Her legs are too short. It is hard for her to climb the mountain.

I know how to get to the other side of the mountain!
Armadillo has sharp claws. She can dig a tunnel!

Dig, Armadillo, dig!
We are almost there!

We made it to the finish line! Here come the other animals. They can run fast. But Armadillo can roll faster.

Roll, Armadillo, roll! Roll across the finish line.

We did it! We won the Rainforest Race! Everyone gets a big ribbon. Hooray for teamwork!